The Sleepover

The Sleepover

Lauren Pearson

Illustrated by
Richard Watson

Orion
Children's Books

ORION CHILDREN'S BOOKS

First published in Great Britain in 2018 by Hodder and Stoughton

1 3 5 7 9 10 8 6 4 2

Text © Lauren Pearson 2018
Illustrations © Richard Watson 2018

A CIP catalogue record for this book
is available from the British Library.

ISBN 978 1 5101 0189 0

Printed and bound in China

The paper and board used in this book are from well-managed forests
and other responsible sources.

Orion Children's Books
An imprint of
Hachette Children's Group
Part of Hodder and Stoughton
Carmelite House
50 Victoria Embankment
London EC4Y 0DZ

An Hachette UK Company
www.hachette.co.uk

www.hachettechildrens.co.uk

For Johnny – L.P.

For Wilf – R.W.

Contents

Chapter 1

Johnny wanted to have a sleepover.

He dreamt of midnight feasts

and spooky stories.

He wanted lots of whispering in the dark and, in the morning, Johnny wanted to have pancakes in his pyjamas.

"You can't have a sleepover,"
said Johnny's big sister Camilla.
"You'll get scared!" Mum agreed.

"I don't think you are big enough yet," she told Johnny. "What if I have to come and get you in the middle of the night?"

Even Johnny had his own *what ifs* about sleepovers: what if his friend Kush didn't sleep with a light on?

What if Christian had bogeys in his bathtub?

What if Johnny lay there in a strange room in a strange house wishing and wishing to come home? He got scared just *thinking* about how scary that would be.

"Invite a friend round here,"
Mum suggested. "You can have a
sleepover in your own room."

But all of Johnny's friends had their
own *what ifs.* No one was brave
enough to have the first sleepover.

Chapter 2

One night Johnny lay in bed listening
to Camilla and her friend giggling
in the room next door. Camilla was
having a sleepover. Again.

"It's not FAIR," said Johnny aloud.
"SO not fair," agreed a small voice
from the darkness.
"Who's there?" cried Johnny.

What if the voice belonged to a
ghost about to slither out from
under the bed? Or an alien with
twenty heads, or—

"Up here, in the corner," said the voice.

A big hairy
spider was
hanging from
the ceiling above
Johnny's bed.

"Camilla is ALWAYS having sleepovers," the spider was saying. "And I've never even had ONE."

"Me neither," said Johnny. Then he remembered that he was talking to a big hairy spider. A big hairy spider that could TALK.

Johnny opened his mouth to scream, but the spider screamed first.

"Keep quiet!" it shouted. "They'll come and squish me!"

As fast as it could, the spider began making its way up to the ceiling.

This spider was just as scared as Johnny was, which made Johnny feel a bit braver.

"Wait," he called out. "I'm sorry. But are you ... venomous?"

"No," said the spider. He looked
confused. "My name is Clark."
"What I mean is," explained Johnny,
"do you bite?"
"No," said Clark. "Do you?"

It turned out that Johnny and Clark had been sharing a room for a long time. Johnny realised it was almost like having a sleepover every single night.

All that was missing were the
midnight feasts and spooky stories.

Suddenly Johnny had an idea.
But could he really have a
sleepover with a spider?

Chapter 3

Clark sat on Johnny's bed in his pyjamas. The spider liked the idea of a proper sleepover but he was nervous, too.

"What if Camilla comes in?" Clark asked. "Last week she tried to stomp on me."

"Don't worry, she's in her bedroom making evil plans," Johnny told Clark.

Every time she had a sleepover,
Camilla and her friends would play
tricks on Johnny. Once they had even
drawn all over Johnny's face with pens
whilst he slept.

"Let's build a tent with my duvet," suggested Johnny.

But they didn't need a duvet.

Above Johnny's head, Clark began to spin the biggest web Johnny had ever seen.

35

Before long there was a silvery tent
hanging down over Johnny's bed.

"Wow," said Johnny. It was the perfect sleepover hideout.

"You can catch flies with it too,"
Clark told him.

Chapter 4

All Johnny had been able to find for their midnight feast was a half-melted chocolate bar. Clark had caught two flies.

Johnny did not want to hurt
Clark's feelings, so he took a
fly and rolled it around in the
chocolate. He gave it to Clark,
and made another for himself.

"One, two, three – GO!"
"Yuck!" They both gagged at the
same time. Clearly Clark found
chocolate as foul as Johnny
found the fly.

"That was the WORST midnight feast in the whole history of sleepovers!" cried the spider. "Wait until I tell my friends I ate chocolate!"

But Clark sounded proud. Johnny was proud too, even though there were bits of fly stuck in his teeth.

Camilla had surely never had anything as gross as chocolate-dipped flies at her sleepovers!

Chapter 5

It was time for spooky stories.

As Clark whispered through the darkness about a pair of giant stinky trainers that went around squishing everyone, Johnny tried hard not to laugh.

But Clark couldn't help giggling at Johnny's story about a headless ghost. To a spider, ghosts are funnier than knock-knock jokes. Johnny started laughing too. Louder than he ever had before.

"Be quiet, Johnny!" shouted
Camilla from down the hall.
"Some of us are trying to have
a sleepover!"

Johnny wished he could tell Camilla that he was having a sleepover too. In fact, when it came to sleepovers, Johnny and Clark were surely winning. Johnny had never had this much fun before. But would Camilla be jealous of a sleepover with a spider?

Camilla was TERRIFIED of spiders.
This gave Johnny another idea;
his sister wasn't the only one who
could make evil plans ...

Chapter 6

It was pitch black when Johnny
and Clark sneaked down the hall
and into Camilla's room.

Camilla and her friend had fallen asleep in a tangle of dolls and sweetie wrappers.

"Ready?" Johnny whispered as he set Clark down on Camilla's desk. "Ready!" cried Clark, with a smile.

Johnny flicked on his torch and held it close behind Clark.

Camilla and her friend opened
their eyes to find the biggest spider
they had ever seen projected on the
bedroom wall. In his shadow, Clark
looked enormous.

"SPIDER!!!!!!!!!!!!!!!"
screamed Camilla.

Johnny had never seen her look so scared. She and her friend crashed into each other as they leapt from their sleeping bags.

"I want to go home!" Camilla's friend shouted.

"I want my muuuuuummmmmmyyyyyy!" cried Camilla.

Johnny and Clark raced back to
their cobweb tent, giggling.

"This is the best sleepover ever!"
Johnny said. All of his *what ifs* had
disappeared in the excitement.

"Let's have another sleepover tomorrow," Clark suggested, "and invite all our friends!"

What are you going to read next?

Don't miss
magic and adventure in the
Three Little … stories